His
Emotions
Released

Poetry Blog: www.amazulugaming.com
Instagram: Onepoeticgamer
Twitch: www.twitch.tv/onepoeticgamer

ISBN 978-0-578-71605-3

Published by
AmaZulu Gaming, LLC

All art work done by
Christopher James Rowland

Final Edition
Printed in the United States of America

Table of Contents

Ludus

Storge

Agape

Philia

Eros

Pragma

Philautia (11:11)

Preface

Waiting for her
is similar to playing the numbers,
I wake up every morning
-hoping-
what I put in won me
the jackpot.

Ludus

I Like You

Let me refer back
to childlike confidence
and use it with romance to say
I like you.
See, there isn't much pressure in that
you could take it or leave it
receive it or refuse to believe it
but no matter your reason
I still like you,
not just with my eyes
although you are fine
mathematically defined
I'm inclined to want to feel your vibe
what's it like inside
as I seek where it is you hide
I can count to five
gonna peek to find where you're at
three words to say that
I like you
in fact, if you like
we can get to know each other, right
might have things in common
so the differences bring light
kisses that equal
Keeping It Simple So Each Soul
feels alright
-aight-
and, if you like me too
I was thinking we might
could talk some time tonight
that is, if you like.

Catch The Vibe

I got,
less than two minutes to impress you
which includes mind, body and soul
so I kiss this flow back up to God
hoping divine intervention gets penned
on these lines,
I'm going from 0 to 60 in six seconds
and looking to see if you can keep up, not draft
since you say you that fast
this must be how you pick pocketed my chest
steady robbin' my heart
yet I somehow caught a vibe some ten years later
but I want to understand what it means,
maybe it wasn't obvious to you
from the look in my eyes
as I failed repeated times
to transition these feelings into words
through casual conversation
but you must have missed the pitch
or my curveball wasn't catchable
and you signaled for some other throw
so let me rework my magic
as my conscious screamed
please get at her
not in attempts to out do those chasing
this is more about questions like
"how do you know" or "how can you tell"
and maybe it was me
but after six straight hours on the verbal exchange

I spent the next four thousand, three hundred
and twenty minutes in-between
there and now wondering might you feel the same
vibe I'm ridin' while watching TV
driving down the road
sitting alone in the dark
laying on green grass under clouds
watching stars in the park
figuring the fact is my opinion
but imagine me trying to process this contradiction
maybe the Universe is listening
and It can point me in the right direction
in my effort to position
you past this associate stage
uping the status to something else I can't gather
cause Musiq said it best when he sang
and I'll paraphrase
that there's no pressure to make you my girlfriend
but you have been on my mind for days
enough to make me fast and ask
the Most High what's the plan
because I'm feeling you so much
I want to innerstand
the mission, this vibe,
my thoughts I can't miss facing
so if you ridin' this same wave
please…please don't leave me complacent
and come catch this vibe.

The Convo

Let's talk
you and I
on this other wavelength,
it's obvious you are meant to
communicate something to me
and I speak through poetry
so let me listen
with my heart
fill you with this motion called
attention,
grateful you waited
debated with self
so Her could understand
divine feminine
no loss because wins are limited
and I'm here with this
stage, this point
this twinkle in your third eye
that's got me seeing repeated 3s
the synergy has me
at the moment of nirvana
and I don't want to run
nor chase anymore
so, let's start the convo.

Mind Frame or Frame of Mind

Since you asked
let me show you how my mind works
eyes thirst a bit much
so trust is a must from inner work
searched my heart to discover the words
song bird I heard and learned
prototypes come in versions like
what my soul feels
and I feel like love again after mirroring within
so let me send this through multiverses,
that's multiple verses
I lurk with and wordsmith this from east to west
and let it rest somewhere between
yoga sets and inter dimensional complex
confess to self so God can place me next
to where you rest
let's, take it to the beginning endlessly
feelings like that on repeat
means lifetimes are infinitely within reach
sheesh, slow down the beat
so you can keep up with this heat
call me so your voice can be my sweets
I eat like soup for the soul
if I'm too much to hold
then push me down and up
til your shoulder and chest have had enough
endurance training to realize
that in the end souls don't need to carried,
they mix like light and dark

ying and yang
complex and plain
since you asked, this is what it's like in my brain
if it's all the same then I hope this energy is
the difference.

Internet Flirt

Not much I can do through an internet picture
don't think you can hear it when I begin to whisper
so I whisper my thoughts on light blue lines
to drive my essence into your mind
can I find a way through electronic air waves
convince you from about 1,000 miles away
that this beat, a rhythm from a soul splice
is just as nice as cool Lipton ice
tea, in summer heat, of 102 degrees
this feeling I'm lining up for perfect symmetry
only if simile, no similar
are the one in a billion chances
that could occur,
on your end, let me spend
the next few moments in retrospect
because hind sight be 20/20
so let me make this an educated guess
regulate the mess
I'm about to cause
treat this like the matrix
slow it down to a pause
yes I'm enthralled, caught before the fall
to usher in the winter
so I can excuse my reason to be up all
in your space, near your face
let me lead
I got you caught out there
but you're safe at my speed
safe cause you're with me
it's just an internet kiss

I didn't mean to mess you up
but this is how I get
switch my focus with heart in check
and hope it's to your liking
a flirt through my computer link
and this was the poem to make it enticing.

Money Shot

What will be, is
so this is that split between art imitating life
and my soul being what I write
it's not like anything else
could compare your atoms to jazzy notes
or float ideas that spoke
to ancient timelines
and how you've been refined through time
that's 9 times three and I'm
on 555 - wait, let me rewind
what signs can I find by aligned symbols
listed back to back, each on top of that
I'm referencing your back tats
fact is, I'm still tasting strawberries
you asked me to last winter
entered in the door marked poets only
since fans only blow air around
my sound can't be filtered
neither can my element, so while you're in yours
I'll paint these lyrics in dawns and sunsets
let's, follow butterflies and one-eyed rhythms
watch you dance to words made beautiful
in days we cherish
life ain't fair but I take the dare since
my living is a lottery and every action is a chance
you can find me when I sleep
so no one else but us can time stamp
this moment, only if you choose
and, I have nothing to lose
so here's to, fade-aways

and ups that lay between they
and this bank shot,
just know that it still counts
even if I don't call it.

Midnight Thoughts

Damn…
I'm really feeling you
like, I'm really digging you
and…
I want to see if you
wouldn't mind feeling this
groove too
see colors move
full circle through the two
of us, want to touch
that boxed wrapped up
kept close
come on,
come feel this mood together
go deeper, see whether
we could glide this cloud nine
you drive, I drive
we ride
this feeling on the inside
butterflies fly
and I,
I…I need this vibe to stay alive
no coincidence, intertwine
your lips so close to mine
can see hereafter reflected in both eyes
yours and mine
paradise in soul ties
my…my sweet…my my…

Storge

Your Smile

Your smile
reminds me of how
the Universe takes sunlight
and pierces rays through
gray clouds.

Angelic,
your heart is next to it
because your smile rests
on this blessing
as you erase hate, pain and sorrow
like an angel itself was sitting beside you.

Reflecting in my eyes
is the joy you bring
in a grin
or even when
you show those pearly whites
that settles me
I feel blessed to see
and know I have the ability
to make the love in you
smile.

Remembering

I place my fingertips
gently onto the sides
of her face,
position her to look
directly into my eyes
past my mind
to hear the sound of the force asking
remember me?

When They See

One of the most
beautiful things I have experienced
is the moment
someone realizes
you love them back.

Wondering If You

I wonder if you think
or dream
of loving me
as much as I do
of you.

In Your Skin

I wish I could be
in your skin
and feel what you feel
when you recognize
and here me say
I love you.

Love on the Low

Due to circumstances
outside of my control
I gotta put this love in a box marked,
"for Her."
See,
or more so
feel this butterfly effect
in my stomach and chest
as I flutter at the moments
you stare directly at me
and dance to rhythms
made by my heartbeat,
I know that smile is for me
and secretly
I whisper to your soul
-I love you-
like when you set your eyes on me
as if I'm prey
and at full speed
you run directly into my arms
for a hug
that's got me feeling as beautiful
as these moments we share
yet,
despite my best intentions
this has to stay in this box
under a lock and key
dangling around my neck
that you somehow keep getting

and I'm beginning to think
this isn't going to ease up
all the intensity
so I'll simply
love you on the low
even though
there's no way to hide the energy
between you
and me.

Beyond the Cortex

Carrying these thoughts
in octaves
by way of electromagnetic energy
so you can feel me through telepathy
cleared my heart so
you could send vibes back to me
universally, listening
picturing what will be
label this
soul searching.

Agape

For Her

Gentleman,
won't claim to be
but if it's meant to be
let me be the one
holding us both ways
-up and down-
heart sounds like African drum beats
for Her
when thinking of Her
and I wonder can She feel it
appreciate it
or am I this
"suppose to be man"
that society created,
because when I falter
will you debate
if this risk called love was worth
the time spent, the moments put together
for the dream of being the one to kiss
and hear me say to you
"go get it baby"
I'm the challenger
causing you to come at me different
causing you to wonder
causing you to think
about me when you should be giving attention
to something else
like I do for you
it's 50/50 or if need be
100 miles per hour

to catch your mishaps
just because,
cause if I'm worth it
you'd know it
despite every odd against me
you should listen to your gut feeling
since we stand on faith
I can be that cut from a different cloth
or the lent in your pocket
either way, it all stands on me being worth
what makes me
-me-
you accepting me as I am
gentle...or just man...
that seeks the better and worse
in you.

Beautiful Is You

I'm going to keep telling you
"you're beautiful"
til it's ingrained in your head
wash your brain with phrases like
damn baby, you're beautiful
and, how wonderfully beautiful it is to feel you
make you confess to a higher being
that this guy keeps repeating
you're beautiful
so that you believe it
daily, no secondly
so between moments of lonely
you'll find beautiful keeping you company
liken this to habits formed in 21 days
moon phase this phrase
you're beautiful
until it erases negative concepts
replaces false positives of self
we'll call this self-help
with a boost
cause you are beautiful
combined with pretty or fine is nice
but beautiful, that's beyond the bone
into that inner you that's actually carried by the soul
it cost you nothing, despite being sold
marketed by society that wants control
but all I know is
you're beautiful, that's right
you're beautiful, that's love
you're beautiful and that's enough
for me.

Wave Length

She's that blue bird
in tune to waves made by high tide
outside here I search for patterns similar
to clothes found hanging in thrift stores
many consider these things has been
but I can remember when
bearing witness to light while lost at sea
made a richer reconnection to
known unknowns
in phases that caused these waves
that make way
I could say
I've waited for this moment
this blue bird I heard chirping,
in a place it shouldn't be
or so I think
maybe this is an astral plane
during a day time nap
in large beach window panes
fingers gripping loose change
more specifically, this dime piece
this time peace
that doesn't equate to monetary value
but I'd give it
to hear that bird sing,
that blue bird sings
like fluid water in my dreams
that carries that same wave

at great lengths
from one end to the other
in my mind,
blue bird.

Inside Out

I can
feel you dancing
in my mind
so beautiful
you are a
form of art
expressed so eloquently
truthfully
voice triggers blues
that soothe, that move
I do, choose to
groove, in rhythm
so beautiful
have to move into
view, intangible energy
touching the inner part of you
telling your soul what it already knew
green spinning in spectrum hue
telepathically sent this
since we're distant
let that vision sink in
it's due,
and I hope
you can feel my mind dancing,
so beautiful.

Listening To You Breathe...
(Read this at a slow pace)

You sound so beautiful
listening to you breathe
knowing it is I
that puts you at ease
Miles Davis plays
and this moment of peace
feels good to experience
with you so close to me
it's early in the morning
and I'm asking God please
how'd I get so lucky
to obtain what I've achieved
and I believe I heard the answer
as you turned to now face me
sighed, a slight moan
you're comfortable
you breathe…
and I'm pleased.

Random Particulars

Moonlight,
when I'm setting
it's your turn to shine
reflection of yours to mine
and I, I prefer your phase in new
when the naked eye can't see
as you blend in with darkness
yet we share the same energy
the same space
holding the same worth
self already knows
I wonder how this goes
as I sit outside the window,
you may never let me in the door
but I won't drop another opportunity
to share love between stars people wish on
it's this balance of water
that heightens emotions that
make it to surface level
what you hold deep
yeah I peep it, from a distance
resistance is futile
and while we on the subject
let me objectify intentions
I'm past the physical cause I listened
what you gettin' is nature speaking to me
reaccepting He through She
dam, now that you "sea"
70% of my make up
isn't makeup, it's made of

what'cha looking for
past and present
not random, in fact particular
and if you let the Sunshine in
we can begin where this poem ends.

Sky Flower

If only she knew how I dream
when looking at her picture
I thank you while thinking of you
6 hours later and I'm still watching you
in this time frame, need this cosmic love
to evaporate then precipitate
and fall onto your face
life cycle so we exist in each element
so everything I do finds me on your mind
in your heart, at the cusp of your soul
I've known what you knew
and others should know
feel this the second before you doze off
and turn on the ground I have a fair chance in,
let's press butterflies together
feel hearts pump energy back and forth
between the reasons we came here in the first place
this realm, this Land of Oz
I model the same feelings
found on Earth and Heaven
if you want it, just come and get it
or maybe is it
we meet somewhere in the sky
over Southern Atlantic water currents
and here…here we'll exchange greetings
lose track of time, you and I
two beautiful orchids in the Universal orchard
some say extasy but we call it
delight.

Philia

Love Both Ways

(read this from top down - pause - then read it from
bottom to top)

poetically
I kiss you
with these words that make love to you
which in essence is me
so that in moments like now
I kiss you
poetically

Perspective with Self

Let me give you life
in these words
heal those wounds I know self can
but I will
because I am able and
you can choose to let me
even though you're powerful enough
to do it yourself,
we know each other's story
and that's why
it's ok for me to do this
to know this force that
made this moment
is as real as the faith
that was birthed by intuition
my darkness is luminous
in your light that clings to shadows
this is what's supposed to be
no fear, no rules
just love, just us
together because we are not alone
and impossible is but a word
no matter how things look
what I believe
you do as well
ascension as phoenix
as a bond from this life force
cycles through on repeat.

Finding Myself

I need affection
as in smooth fingers stroking back skin
with moist slow kisses
sniffing scents of body emissions
so relaxed it's as if we become the breeze
made by an angel sneeze
I need, affection
as beautiful as November sunny days
in the country
made innocent in early afternoon coastin'
by Sunday driving,
slow enough to appreciate
love.
I-am in need-of affection
that's built on blind eyes
depends on deaf ears
using a mute voice
to understand the limits of self,
when it begins
when hope ends
mends when broken
listens when spoken
I need affection,
beyond roots of motherlands
chains of depressions
found deep in wells
like morning dew drops
running cool down my soul
as beads of bliss

this is the joy
of affection that I need
found only in Her
that knows She
can find the same
in me.

K-I-S-S-I-N Me

In my dreams I can see you
you love to be
K-I-S-S-I-N Me.
Two sometimes three
I like it when she
K-I-S-S-I-N Me.
On the chest, on the face
both left and right cheeks
K-I-S-S-I-N Me.
Really sweet on the lips
best believe a special treat
K-I-S-S-I-N Me.
Be it French or a peck
transferring energy
K-I-S-S-I-N Me.
What's this, I hear my name
She's gently calling
K-I-S-S-I-N Me.
She loves to call me B-Dot
Poetic or Billy
in-between I call her sweet thing
sometimes it's teasing me
she'd agree, all for me
I'm glad it's all for free
K-I-S-S-I-N Me.

By The Thought of You

I took pleasure in Her voice
similar to cool breezes in mid summer
longing, fresh inhales in my nostrils
which left lust evaporating
in morning secrets.
I love you
on the tip of my inner most feelings,
it's beyond dangerous the rules
that are having to be broken
for my being doesn't set standards
it births impossibilities
while toying with perfection
living in manifested dreams
here, come drink from this chalice
filled with liquid risk
sun kiss the drops that drip
like tears off lips that
were cooled by the thoughts of you,
I flow deep in octaves
that move slow to the Universe's rhythm
Goddess please…please don't leave
I find You to be the need I've sought
essential and innate
like breathing
speak easy,
as I etch this into my forever
to remember Her completely
when all else is made to be forgotten.

Musical Note

She walked in my life through a DM
and now I can't stop writing hymns about her
to her, dreaming up repeated forehead endearments
intimately, done repeatedly
sending them through 4D transmissions
part this mist with your spirt
so my aquatic ways can kindle
polar opposite of you
come shotgun smoke lifeblood
into my subconscious
with the softest of lips,
and I wish on this attraction of law
that I'm worth the attention
surreal, for real
in balance like double nose piercings
while you pull that off
please put this on
my coat of warmth and safety
put down my arms
so the only war fought
is you falling into them
gently, I believe the tears that slip
from my eyes at night
is from the joy of watching you breathe
believe, this ain't deep
this just is, be it
as I inhale you and find comfort
like faces buried in freshly washed sheets
find our way to pleasure
whether or not it's spiritual

or on human vibrations
I'm thanking whatever deity or energy
you believe in for this moment
because we've lived to experience
what was agreed upon
before leaving each other from that place
where time doesn't exist.

Tall Glass of Water

Glass chilled at about 42 degrees
sparkling – ice – cold – water
they say I need 8 cups of it
but this one...
this one will do,
even when she's lukewarm
and packaged in bottles labeled
Alipine Spring or Nature's Crop,
I'm only concerned about it being natural
out the brook and running deep
through mother Earth,
I said out the brook and running deep
through mother Earth
or in forms of drops made way from heaven
it's all beautiful
no matter the shape but more important,
the taste
and I'm wondering
if I – can get – a drink
make no mistake
she is not ice nor vapor
even though it's H20 that compounds her
I am in need of that quick rush
the one where
the only thing that will satisfy one's thirst
is a kiss of dew made true
by divine inspiration
don't mix this like integration
this is untapped, no tonic

right next to the holy
-water-
and if I may
I'll like a nice tall glass
of that natural – fresh – bliss.

Eros

Now That's "Liquid"

Thinking when I say
she's wet
is purely sexual
gives me reason to believe
why you don't understand her flow
how her currents
curve the mathematics
in her design
watch me go to her mind
to drink thoughts
while refreshing my soul.

In My Feels

If you were here now
physically
I'd make love to you,
not like the typical thought
as that's a given,
I need to enter parts of you
that's hidden from view
feel that urge that makes it so
you find yourself unable to lay still
in the feels
and it would only feel better
with you here
breathing lightly into my skin
not wanting to move
holding the back of my head
laying in-between legs
lovingly embracing what was a dream
now a moment we need
and I believe this might just be
the prelude to something magical
yet oh so real
in a time it felt worthy enough
to fall from heaven into
your arms.

Massage Therapy

Deposited deep in my mind banks
are the curves and features of your face
know that
-this-is-love-making-
not just some sexual advance
I'm about to make you want me
with my fingers, like magic
soothing your skin like cubes of ice
on high humidity days
taking temporary control of your whole frame
your body is the art I'm crafting
repeated motions of coordinated therapy
from my hands
to your thigh
then the calf
on to your foot and toes
and, you seem pleased
cause when you breathe
it's slow and deep
with pauses in-between
got me whispering
"you like that?"
and that smirk on your face tells me
I need not ask
so I react by moving towards your center
where the button of your belly has been pierced
and this kiss
it's a bit extra
but, it's what sets me apart
sets you on fire

a desire
so strong only I can quench your thirst
which arm do you want first,
as you watch what I do with my hands
your focus goes in and out
sometimes staring at me
sometimes eyes closed
I know your half way to heaven
but wait, there's more
now turning you over
feeling those blues that are parked between
your shoulder blades melt away
ecstasy with out the pill
thrills without the kill
in a circular motion
we can do this with oil or lotion
I like it with peppermint scent
as it feels strong
and I carry on from the upper side of your mainland
down to the peninsula
where problems seem to lay
and it is my pleasure to clear out the bay
hey baby,
you sure we don't already have matching tattoos
cause my love is now etched into you
from the top to the bottom of your frame
to the inside of your brain
and I
didn't need sex to show you my specialty
to show you
-this-is-love-making-

just a forgotten piece
that most use as a mere tool
and ooooooo,
let me now hush so that you
can go...
to sleep...

Love Music

I now know
what it means to make love music
by piecing together memories
then letting go of control
as the soul takes over
this is how we learn each other's code
feel colors in love
touch sound with eyes
recognize so many words from silence
reset in and out of existence
this divine flow
so comfortable with you
alone, with you
I need to be with you
to dream state our personal landscape
what we've waited around for
that moment, this circumstance
the experience of love music
orchestrated by
you and I.

When You Say

I like the way you call my name
a devious sounding vocal,
"Bil-ly"
and when I comment on it
you deny it and say my name no more
or, not until the moment arises
for you to say it
and repeat it,
"Billy."
You get excited
from my joke, my sarcasm
when I pick at you….
Billy!
I laugh,
knowing I've stimulated, irked you
say it again,
Billy!
I think you like
how it rolls off your lips
as if you practice in your mind saying
my name
"Billy…Billy…Billlly,"
yeah really
I like it when you say my name,
let me hear it again
"Billy."

Peach Like

I want to know what that taste like,
like, what's it taste like
to you.
I mean, describe it to me
go deep inside
overwhelm me with your emotions
place it into words
cause my mind to stimulate
make my mouth salivate
make me want to taste
looking,
see it in your face
through those eyes
how beautiful it is
as you glow
warm,
feels like music
in body reactions
and I'm asking
what it taste like
that peach right
let me hear it,
from you.

Intimate Salute
(Or in other words Affectionately Smooch)

This act is without reason
so disconnect your logic during this kiss
this moment of humans creating with lips
as moods will ride high
fill lows, both placed on recycle
and I-like-you,
enough to gaze into moments
observing as words are mouthed
or, rims curve out math
that I add and subtract
causing multiple emissions
of oxytocin, soft muscular folds when
gently felt breath tween
short pauses at crosses of chins
slight lean in, pecks between grins
and the blend of power begins
sending us off on journeys
made way by butterflies
reverse back to me cause you like
eye, to eye, open wide
despite lids being closed
we're neck deep in our minds
and as skies line, we're aligned
let it be,
as we intimately salute
it's balanced harmony.

Pragma

333

I lay in thought
because I stand for truth
and the truth of this matter is
I can't shake you from cognition
spirit moved
and I find this craving
to be in your conceptions
as worldly explanations
logically tell me turn away
but I can't help to notice you
when the wind moves curtains
from the windows I look in and out of
facing soulful pandemics
I attach my branch to yours
to help you take root,
I agree that self-care is a necessity
but if you heard my soul speak
you'd understand my need
to assist in sowing
any of your ripped cloth pieces
no, I'm not obligated
I choose to do so
in the face of laws that dictate
matrix type human reactions
but I'm defined by anomalies
as beliefs always show the intention
hope your heart has turned on available senses
as I lay in dreams throughout the day
in search of you.

Scientifically Spiritual

I light bend
relative to theory
I find you in that umbra
squinting,
so I use higher self to navigate
where you store secrets
seek this or that
gloves off because
time is not relevant
spin like spheres through cycles
in totality
transport this energy in waves found
mechanical, electromagnetic
-spirit-
from here to there
where you are
we're none minus one
I hope you catch that math
speak universal as science is dropped
using corrective lens
so your mind's eye can see me as vapors
wet but still exist in heat
-and-
I know you've never read
a love poem like this before
at least not one that's
from me, to you
green - red - blue
communicating deep in silence
while nature sings.

Kisses of the Third

Thinking of the past
and my mother's well wishes
giving me love through
third eye kisses,
a love now forgotten
or at least pain I'm no longer missing
remember giving her soul upliftment
from third eye kisses,
not to be found wanting
but I could use it, telepathically given
twin has yet to appear
to give me those third eye kisses,
so let's tap into the Universe
have Spirit focus in on my position
clear the clutter so I can receive
continuous third eye kisses.

At 7.83 Hz

She wanted to go to sleep
in my blanket
scented in memories
wrap herself in my past
and enjoy my present
absorb my essence
taste my ambiance
communicate with me
through convalescence
in relation to
the mother that created me
with the foundation of my birthright
in her belly
give this seed
the other half of greatness
take this energy
in sound mind and mesh it with
hearts, start the bloodline
of freedom in Heaven on Earth
this worth can be found
in our embodiment
when we met
past the moon and sun
from the same One that blew breath
in galaxies
no fallacy to be found
or lost, this cost the time endless
and in this shell, she'll find
night that provides light
to the right of evolution

in the language of universal love
as I awoke
I give her this kiss
while birds and the sunrise
sing together
she breathes so softly
directly into my benevolence
and it is here
you'll find me.

Moonlight

Her thoughts sativa, my flow is indica
inhale and my words are into the
subconscious, either way it's looked at
we're both in outer space
and higher than I care to admit
her house sits 4 down from mine
and I find that time moves like water
maybe this could be a sign
fixated on her creation
past finite elemental mathematics
and into energy that shines
in darkness, let's spark this
roll up this paper I'm scribing on
supernova the electrons in her mind
physics got me being physical
urban legend our love in reality
level 3 vision is far from blind
rubies in her eyes
vulnerable, emotional
if I knock, when will you let me inside
unspoken speeches as you stare at me
secrets healed closely
in a world that's full of lies
combine the truth with the facts and you
get a love like that
wrote this on a Thursday
so by Monday maybe you'll react
these persuasive verses nurse
that mood, relax the attitude

no need to be insecure, I won't ignore you
stretch those long legs across my latitude
peruse the news as we rebirth the cool on cruise
and, what do I do since you currently choose
to be a lock
watching on high form full to new
this beautiful glowing rock.

Balanced Intimacy

At times my rays
need not be those of heat
she seeks reflections held smooth
as light from moons
fluctuates in palms slid across her face
the tofu of calm
essential,
Spirit supersedes the mental
just like music fused it so
the universal language we speak
is pure mathematics
they see it, we be this
progress of power not found on Earth
literally plucking words
out of space
into this place
on to this page
like moon phases
cycle rebirths in
27 days 7 different ways
amazed you daze me
in 43 distinct forms of praise
I paid attention so ying and yang get laid
as 6 and 9 make circles, lights fade
behave, as when morning comes
we can push the button labeled repeat,
as tonight in my arms
she stays.

Sunset Dance

She dances in rhythm to this song
hips moving in such a motion
that I'm in a trance
your soul knows how bad I desire you
how I want to
move with you
grab you by the waist and just
move,
maybe I should step back for a second
I enjoy watching you
seeing the algebraic equations
flowing in this sunset heat
just enough sweat to make her body parts glisten
my mind is gone
but you keep playing songs with my soul,
I need to touch you
but don't want to pause the moment
and rewind won't find the time spent
looking for this vision
this, piece of utopia
called mate
different time, different place
and maybe I'm checking you,
listen queen
I'm getting ready to merge into you
cause then there's no go back
no what if
and maybe then it will be for me
you dance

for me
you sing
on me
you place your head
in my heart
to dance
to its beat
then, it will be
we...
dancing in the sunset.

Philautia (11:11)

Spiritual Makeup

Natural is a beauty all its own
and I found myself
casting stones on female physicality
-meanwhile-
I covered my spirit
with a mask
and layered societal threads
over my body
to hide behind learned egotistical fears,
and as I played judge and jury
on you repeatedly
I executed my own self daily
letting my life be dictated
and held hostage
with tunnel vision perspective,
so I say to you Cover Girls
this Wonder Boy apologizes
for putting you in a box.

Find and Seek

She descended upon me
as rainfall
and I absorbed Her in
like elemental crystals
blended twin in acoustic instrumentals
lips set to whistle
you can hear our song
meanwhile,
earth and water mix
feeding roots of emotions
deep in, life like
branches of trees outstretched
this is the part
where you and I meet
eclipsed over stars
in constant rebirth
eternal, and
remember I'm going to always find
my way to you
or you to I
just today it was by
falling rain.

Water to Bare, Water to Spare

I whisper words into my element
seeking peace and relief,
listening…being…
that flow, that drip, that push
filled in,
I whisper this sonnet
in hopes it evaporates and elevates
then makes way across skylines
to rain this poem into your earth
if you're giving attention
as I did when I listened
to vibrations in distance
like 4K vision in kilometers,
uplifted.
I thought of gifting this to you
despite the lack of said compatibilities
as I fit into shape of any place
hoping to be absorbed then transmuted
let this lyric move from mind frame
to spirit,
so the whisper moves from
voice to essence
something you can use
or
give away,
either way
as long as the next time you cry
you recognize that I
have generated in liquid form
through you.

Something Like Harmony

I think of the feelings felt
when merging energies
under the sound of one's voice
the choice to create in the space
of oneness,
harmonizing into the blues with rhythm
discovering brand new in notes
kept on tablets
share this similarity as a card match
two of the same difference
we're cosmic, toxic
total opposites of normal definitions
I observe so you can tell I listen
nonexistent are lengths and measurements
described as moments
you're lucid, I reflect translucent
esoteric convoluted love surges this
while you putting oceans in skies
I move rocks through sun lit moon rides
skinny dipping in pools that leak from your mind
high on lyrics sounding off by the look in your eyes
and, these are the feelings I
felt when crossing energies
in oneness with
-you-

Create Light

Let's create light
between you and I
beyond the joining of thighs
and the looking in eyes,
be that love
the feeling
that whisper saying
we were made to fit
ask me can I sense that
and I just know,
flow that has us in dimensions
far, far away from here
and I'm there
with you
exploring mysteries we didn't even know
we wanted
fresh, like present day
fond as if a loving memory
cycling in time
let's place absolutes inside out
of forever
however we like
let's create
light.

I'm Too, To You

I find myself
enraptured to all of you
parts of you finite and infinite
I never knew I could
create love with a voice
or merge into nature
with my soul
feet grounded in earth
this worth is better than
my limited human perspective
so I sit next to subconscious
that speaks multiverse languages
and I find myself
adrift inside of you
where I feel I should be
alone, yet, with you
mirroring love is love
tags free
so into, or am I unto
to you
covering both our perspectives
I'm left with this right there
over here where
we're, no, we be and were
clearly lines blur
or it may be
that maybe I'm too,
to you.

Forever is Now

My connection to you is based on the soul
so I know you are the one
two, three and infinite,
and my efforts to reach this understanding
can be clouded by my human imperfection.
I sometimes think you'll leave me
what if you deceive me
what if you don't believe me
this, is mental hell
knowing I can't rely on feelings
even though it's through emotions
I receive the greatest of highs
I realize that
it's going to take more than life experiences
to appreciate the mere essence of what I whisper
I prefer sometimes to fish where I can see
but this connection is vast like oceans
where man can't break certain depths
but we know there is existence
deep in parts that only the Most High can see
you'll find me resting with your being,
and at times
I wish you could understand these poetic phrases
these, attempts to make limited words
express a bigger meaning
I know you can sense
I'm going way out with this one
but make no mistake
this is the place where
99% of the Earth's population

will stop trying to comprehend
and just clap their hands saying
that this poem is real good,
seeing that I'm misunderstood
and unconcerned with their appreciation
it's the reckoning they not facing
so I,
connect the dots
pin point mathematics and meditate
so that I can penetrate these things with strings
in order to connect mind, body and soul together
however imperfect,
so that when the time comes that
we lose body and mind
they would have already been captured in spirit
thus our souls will always know
each other…
forever.

About The Author

Billy Williams, Jr. was born to write poetry. Poetically knows as B-Dot and OnePoeticGamer, the life as a poet all started because of a girl back in 7th grade. Seeing he had a gift with words, he began to use his energy to produce poetry that spoke to various genres.

Hailing from Raleigh, North Carolina, Billy is a poet, educator, coach, gamer, streamer, content creator and inspirer. His Emotions Released is Billy's third book of published poetry, with more poetry books to be released in the near future. Billy has been published in several different poetry collections, most notably to him:
The Black Scholar and Broken Streets.

If you want to find out more information about Billy's upcoming books, you can contact him by way of e-mail at onepoeticgamer@amazulugaming.com or sending a message to him from the following website www.amazulugaming.net. If you wish to know more about his gaming/streaming life, check him at www.twitch.tv/onepoeticgamer.

Social Media Contacts

Poetry Blog: www.amazulugaming.com
Instagram: Onepoeticgamer
Twitch: www.twitch.tv/onepoeticgamer

AmaZulu Gaming, LLC

Poetry Books Written By One Poetic

Poetic Superhero

Everybody is looking for a hero. Poetic Superhero is here for you.

The I prElude I (ebook only)

In order to find we, HE must find himself before finding SHE.

His Emotions Released

This is written for Her…I'm glad I finally got Her attention.

School Dad

Poetry inspired by 16 years of working as an educator in elementary, middle and high school.

the Book of HER

33 poems for HER

Poetic Flows - A Book of Rhymes (upcoming 2021)

When I feel the flow, I let go with words.

Excommunicated (A Bard's Tale)
(2022 Release)

Leftover Love Poems (2022 Release)

Sometimes you'll get things humanely wrong just so
your soul can get right

Odds and Ends (2022 Release)

<u>Spoken Word By One Poetic</u>

Blue Room Mix Tape
(upcoming soon)